HERO'S
WELCOME

Maryann—
Happy reading
to my dear friend.
Sharon
June 5, 2019

By Sharon Durken

ISBN: 9781098994112

Edits & Cover Design & Layout by:
solfire@phoenix-farm.com

*Author's Note: the story in this book is presented over many time
periods, not flashbacks, some memories, mostly being narrated from different
times. Therefore I have experimented with the verb tense used. My editor and I
have settled on each section giving you the feel that best reflects the character at
the time they are telling that part of the story. Grammar purists should forgive us
in the name of artistry. This note is to let readers know the verb tenses used are
purposeful.

DEDICATION

Always first...my sons.

LAUREL

Today, when I stepped onto Main Street from the deep quiet of my antique store, Peddler's Paradise, it felt like I was walking straight into the five o'clock sun. At five o'clock on a late fall day in Clover, Wisconsin, the sun hangs just across the road from the Dutch Colonial farmhouse I arrived at as a young girl with secrets to hide and memories that are still alive like silent shadows in my life.

Before heading home I'll stop at Sorrel's General Store. Victoria arrives tomorrow for a visit, the first in a year. I've missed my beautiful, blonde daughter and want everything to be perfect, which means picking up extra coffee for the visit. I have mixed feelings about this visit: excited, yet nervous because she's not coming alone. She's bringing a man along; she claims this is a serious visit.

Leaving the smells of the fifty-year-old market behind, I pushed through Sorrel's eight-foot door and see a blue flat-bed truck pull to a stop across the street.

"Evening Laurel, bit chilly. You want a ride home?" Doug Marsh leaned from the cab. Doug drills wells, he's a handsome man; quiet, kind, and thoughtful with thick, salt and pepper hair.

"Thanks, Doug, I wore a heavy sweater today and want to walk." He shrugged his shoulders. I've known Doug since he bought an antique chest from Peddler's Paradise. Over the years he's offered more than rides home. I've used those rides and I've grilled him about his time in Vietnam during our travels. Somehow, I don't feel guilty about accepting or declining his offers.

Tucking the coffee and a book under my arm, I head west. A quarter of an hour ago I left my shop to pick up a library book with information on the antique poison ring I'd bought from an out-of-state dealer who stopped by the shop. Its ornate carving and dusky stone fascinated me.

I checked the shop's door lock out of habit. Lots of habits develop when one lives alone . . . but not so long ago I didn't live alone. My daughter, Victoria, warmed the corners of my heart and house whenever she came home from boarding school. When she left for college it was hard, but it was the next logical step for her and me. I had never really lived alone since that autumn day so many years ago.

I decide to fetch the ring to compare with ones pictured in the library book.

I entered Peddler's Paradise. The smell of old wood, fresh linens, and dried rose petals combined to encircle me with comfort. An explosion of baby's breath, escaping from straw baskets reached out to me in the semi-darkness. Skirting a relic of picket fence, I maneuvered down the aisles between vibrant quilts, tall wardrobes, starched white gowns from the early 1900s, and a baby pram filled with lacy linens. From the ceiling dangled an old sleigh, a row of straight-backed chairs, and garlands of dried flowers. I loved the magical feeling of walking around the store in the semi-light. Every corner was alive with the ghost of another era. I opened the safe, fetched the ring, and re-locked the shop.

The mile stretch toward home invited me like beckoning fingers reaching out to hurry my journey. The road dipped before starting a gentle rise toward the west. Just past my house it hooks toward the north and flattens out as it marches toward Blakely, sixteen miles away.

The chilly fall wind gusts were curling around my ears. Pulling the collar of my heavy, cable-knit sweater close, I walked that last stretch faster than usual. As I trudged the familiar road from town toward home, brown and rust fallen leaves swirled around my feet, stirring the memories that brought me to this place. The wind blew the scent of burning leaves from the Hollis' place down the road. Ever since that autumn at St. Genevieve Girl's School I can't stop the flood of memories that comes with the smell of burning leaves. I've thought about how I'll tell Victoria about that time in my life but hope that time will never arrive. The memories come rushing back with the smell of burning leaves.

LAUREL - 1967

It was homecoming 1967 and we girls at St. Genevieve's scurried in excitement with anticipation of boarding the buses Friday afternoon for the football game at the nearby boys' school. Several nuns and staff joined the girls on the bus for this special outing with an eye toward protecting their innocent charges. The girls at St. Genevieve's were kept safe behind a tall wrought iron fence that surrounded the campus nestled at the edge of Clover, but the tall fence didn't keep us isolated from what was happening outside the walls. Following dinner in the long dining hall each evening, we rushed to the twenty-one-inch television in the lounge to watch Walter Cronkite solemnly deliver news of the dead and dying from Vietnam into our impressionable lives.

To further our education, each day in history class Mr. Mills, Victor, as we girls swooningly called him in our dormitory rooms, lectured us about current and past wars. He drew parallels to the war in Southeast Asia and how it still impacted the present day. Not wanting to appear naive, we listened, read newspapers, and adopted Mr. Mills' attitudes and beliefs in all affairs past and present.

Each of the students was required to hold a job on campus. My job brought me to Mr. Mills' classroom to apply as his assistant; he insisted on one who was interested in history and that was definitely me. His voice at first lulled me as he talked easily about our favorite subject, history. I sat mesmerized as he went on about the war in Southeast Asia. But slowly it became the timbre of his voice and the low resonance of his deep rumbling laughter flowing like lava that caught me. Looking into his blue eyes I became lost in emotions I did not understand. I began to hunger for the times his hand would slide slowly from my shoulder down my back or rest easily on my arm.

Victor had spent his first years teaching in the local public school and said that after that he wanted a smaller, more select audience of students. He got the job at St. Genevieve's from Monsignor Hilly, president of the school. The Monsignor happened to be the uncle of Victor's wife. Thus, Victor Mills arrived at St. Genevieve. His teaching certificate allowed him a deferment from joining the thousands of men his age heading to Vietnam.

"Laurel," he checked over his shoulder then bent close to my ear. His breath caressed my cheek. "I must confess to you," his eyes locked onto mine, "for all I talk about the nobility of war, if I got drafted, I'd go to Canada. I couldn't, wouldn't kill. I don't believe this war is right and I'd denounce my citizenship to prove my convictions, nothing could make me go to Vietnam."

Because he called this honor and felt so strongly, I felt strongly too and joined him and other students on Saturday mornings to march in protest of the war. I never stopped to analyze my own feelings because as a sixteen-year-old, I followed Victor's thinking. His beliefs and goals were mine.

I wished Victor's wife was ugly or an angry shrew to justify my role in what happened next. She was neither. As choir director and music teacher, like a spring flower she was bright as a cheerful bouquet. The girls in the dorm imitated her hairstyle and manners, all except me. The closer Victor and I became, the more difficult it was to watch her tender expressions as she directed the Ave Maria on Sundays. My involvement with Victor was like slowly sinking into a warm bath. Now, I see the innocence and dependence that made up the sixteen-year-old me. Innocent until that dark Wednesday when Sister Eloise entered Victor's classroom where I was correcting papers.

"My dear," Sister Eloise murmured as she stepped closer and clutched my hand. "Laurel, look at me, you must be strong." I felt panic and looked around the room, as if for an escape. "There's been an accident; your parent's tour bus collided with a truck and overturned." I tried to swallow as my throat tightened. "They were both killed, Laurel." The nun held me as I struggled to breathe. The day stopped with that news.

My parents had been musicians and travelled with a band called Renowned; mother as singer and father on steel guitar. They were on the road most of the time. Until I started school I toured with them. Once I turned six they enrolled me in St. Genevieve's boarding school and I saw them only about four times a year. They bought a house, only six miles from St. Genevieve, to be close to me, but they were seldom there. A housekeeper stayed with me during school vacations when they were away, which was most of the time.

BEGINNING OF THE END

The sun was setting and the school visitors and classmates departed after offering their condolences on the loss of my parents. The housekeeper had retired to bed, Victor and I were alone in the kitchen. Victor sat at the kitchen table staring silently into his lukewarm coffee. I alternated between bouts of tearful silence and recalling memory scraps of my parents.

I was trying to grasp what had happened, but only one thing seemed real, Victor. And the way he looked at me.

He reached for my hand as he stood and without planning, I moved toward him. He held me and I clung to him. At first his arms comforted, but comfort shifted to more. No boy had kissed me until Victor held my face in his hands and kissed my lips. No one had touched my body until that night. I drank in his comfort to assuage my grief. I accepted his lovemaking and it quickly became the focus of my life.

I've often asked myself if I was also to blame for what followed. Victor filled my hours first with comfort and then passion as the months passed until, as lovers do, we became careless. Because my house was close to St. Genevieve it was an easy escape for us. I became greedy for more of this man who had become the entire universe of my life.

"Victor, love me, love me forever. Promise you won't ever leave me."

"Of course I'll love you forever, silly. But we have to be careful because of my wife and my job. What if the Monsignor found out? It would be awful, but my sweet thing, don't worry." His breath came in staccato gasps as I raised up, letting the waves of my red hair weave a pattern across his heaving chest. He loved my youth, that I knew. He talked often about young girls and their budding breasts. I was glad my figure was thin and breasts small. As long as I stayed this way, I was sure Victor would be with me forever. But…

"Laurel, tomorrow is my wife's birthday and I won't be able to see you."

That hurt. I pleaded and cried until he agreed to stop by directly after class, before he took his wife out for dinner. I was filled with victory. I thought I'd won and knew it was only a matter of time before he would leave his wife for me. Although he forbade me to talk about the future, I knew without a doubt we would spend the rest of our lives together.

The next day I skipped Latin to hurry home and prepare for Victor's visit. I decided to make myself irresistible. I found a thin negligee in my mother's chest, pulled my thick red hair up and fastened it with pearls. Her clear sling-back heels were big and I tripped as I hurried to answer the doorbell and entice Victor to skip the birthday all together. But, when I opened the door, it wasn't Victor.

My visitors stared at my nakedness through the sheer gown as they moved into the parlor and sat in grim silence. I ran up to my room. The heavy footsteps of Sister Eloise echoed on the steps behind me. My make-up was smeared from my tears. Sister brought me a warm wash cloth and helped me into a sweater and skirt, then silently waited for me to descend the stairs to the waiting group, following me down in more grim silence.

I sat in stillness with my shame. Each looked at me and then at each other with jagged glances; all except Victor's wife who cried and twisted a handkerchief in her hands.

How could I warn Victor? I knew he would think of some lie to cover our secret if only I could warn him in time. Or, maybe this was when he would renounce his wife and tell all of them he loved me and wanted to be with me forever.

A shriek of chimes interrupted the silence.

"Answer the door Laurel," the Monsignor ordered. Sister Eloise looked at me, her features frozen in the same ice that encircled my heart. Slowly I rose from the sofa. Before I reached the door, it was opened by Victor, who swept in, catching me in a twirl.

"Hello, little darling, are you ready for some loving before I have to dash off?" Then he cast me away from him as he took in the figures of his wife, the Monsignor, and three nuns.

Would I ever see Victor Mills again? The girls from school called the next day to ask why I wasn't there. They told me Mr. Mills stopped to collect his personal belongings. His hair was cut short and he was wearing an Army uniform.

Private Victor Mills had volunteered for Vietnam. They said he'd volunteered because it was his duty to serve his country. I was sent away at the end of the term to live with my Aunt Ruth.

LAUREL WALKS HOME

Today I shiver as I pull my sweater close. The memories of my yesterdays spill over me like warm honey. Already I'd walked over Possum Creek Bridge and was starting up the hill. I wonder why these memories are so vivid after all these years, then wonder why it surprises me.

Hasn't Victor consumed my thoughts and dreams throughout much of my life? At this time of year they seemed to come alive with renewed vigor. I could taste the salty flavor of his skin. It seems only this morning I felt the silk of his wavy hair, looked into his eyes, and felt the demanding roughness of his kisses.

The memory of our long-ago words intrude, and I remember how I begged him to be with me and swore eternal love.

Amazing how Victor stayed with me in my memories, day after day, and night after night. He was never far from my heart. Later, much later, I contacted the Veteran's Department to study the long lists of MIAs, wounded, and dead. Searching for his name and praying never to find it.

I stayed close to St. Genevieve long after I graduated from high school and college and even after Aunt Ruth passed away. I'm still living within the shadow of the school in Clover. All those years I waited, thinking Victor would surely return to me. Each day I awoke hoping this might be the day he'd find me, that he'd come knocking on the door or enter the antique store.

I left my forwarding address at St. Genevieve's, but no one ever called, and I couldn't go there to ask about him. My eyes constantly searched the road for a strange car.

I've waited for twenty-two years as of this month. Now I feel the same wind teasing my face with a touch of cool, then flitting warmth as I wipe the tears away with the back of my hand. I recall stepping off the bus into my new world in Clover in 1967. The wind caught Aunt Ruth's wispy hair causing it to escape from her pillbox hat as she waited for me to exit the bus.

"Child, you look ready to blow away, let's load your bags and head home."

My new home was to be with Aunt Ruth in Clover, only ten miles but years away from St. Genevieve. I'd only met Aunt Ruth, my mother's sister and only living relative, at my parent's funeral. I knew my parents were estranged from family since they left college, eloped, and devoted their lives to music on the road. I wondered why they'd isolated me from this short, smiling woman. Her warmth drew me to her at the funeral and encircled me now.

Aunt Ruth maneuvered around the bus station, gingerly stepping around the duffle bags and soldiers on their way to Vietnam. I avoided looking at those uniformed shapes, although I could feel their eyes appraising me. The olive camouflage tore into my memories like artillery, ripping my life apart. I thought I could hear one of Victor's poems as it reverberated through the bus station loudspeaker:

> I'll tell you a story
> About my little Laurie,
> Copper hair and eyes so green,
> Cutest titties I've ever seen.

I quickly looked around the station wondering if anyone heard my sobs as I remembered the silly and sweet times with Victor.

Aunt Ruth's smile led me from the station to her 1953 cream and brown Chevy, then the ride to the Dutch colonial house which I still call home.

My aunt settled into a rose floral chair. Her feet lifted in unison onto the tufted ottoman. A wood stove hummed in the corner. "Laurel, now that life has brought us together tell me what has happened since your parent's funeral. The nuns called and said you were to live with me; the lawyers sold the house and here you are."

I set down the chamomile tea, walked to the window, and for the first and last time talked about Victor. I unloaded my emotions along with the entire story. Ending with the biggest secret yet, "That's not all, Aunt Ruth. You may want to throw me out, but I'm having Victor's baby." That last bit was blurted out to end my outburst.

Those loving arms reached toward me and held me through an hour of sobs and later childbirth pains. Quietly, on Victoria's fourteenth birthday, Aunt Ruth slipped away. At first I had felt anger at my parents for isolating me from this wonderful woman for so many years, but as time passed I came to understand that her life had been fulfilled caring for me and loving Victoria and that my parents had been too chaotic to mesh well into Aunt Ruth's life. My aunt expressed her kindness by willing me her most prized possession, Peddler's Paradise, a successful antique store which I have operated ever since.

My walk is over, I check the house, all is ready for my guests. I'm restless and walk with my dog, Goldie, then spend the night tossing, unable to sleep.

I'm not sure how I feel about expanding our family of two. Since Aunt Ruth died it has been just Victoria and me. Maybe now was the time to bury my ghosts and be ready for the next chapter.

Or so I thought.

VICTORIA'S VISIT

As the door flies open a gust of cold November enters mixed with the warmth of Victoria's smile. We twirl around the kitchen in each other's arms. Breathless, we stop next to a tall, thin man whose beard, tinged with silver, matches his pony-tail. As he extends his left hand I see his empty right sleeve pinned up neatly with a large, shiny safety pin. His resonant voice rakes my flesh.

"I'm David Mills, Victor David Mills, call me Dave."

Victor...my world explodes.

Our eyes lock as disbelief spills forth from mine and confusion from his. How did I survive with my fingers frozen in his hand those first moments? Thanks to Goldie, who got excited and knocked over a basket of apples they rushed to collect, I used the time to escape to the bathroom.

I study the face of a woman who seemed a stranger in the last moments. *Did Victor recognize me?* I'd seen confusion as he struggled for recognition and feared by now he'd know it was me.

I ran my fingers through my hair, which was always thick and long, the deep auburn now streaked with gray. I studied the face in the mirror for telltale signs of the young woman I'd been when he last saw me. Had he come back to me finally? I became confused and frightened at the implications of this strange situation.

"Mother, where is the picture of my father, the one taken before he left for Vietnam?" She searched for the picture of a lonely looking man in uniform I'd rescued from a junk box at the antique store and passed off as her dead father all these years. I'd even named him Robert and woven fabricated tales of our brief and undying love. I explained our different last names, hers in honor of Aunt Ruth, and mine the one from my parents. I kept that name hoping Victor would find me one day, but not like this.

"It's on the bookcase by the window," I said.

Victoria picked up the photograph and sat by Victor, *David, Dave.* A race was taking place in my head and the roar of Grand Prix engines drowned out Victoria's voice.

From beside my wingback chair I lifted some quilting. While pretending to work I studied the man. At the same time I felt him study me. I had no doubt now that he knew who I was.

The years had touched him with an artist's brush. Where once I'd seen careless strength, now I saw a frailness as if something had sucked the core from his soul. As he reached to brush a stray hair from Victoria's face, his hand lingered on her cheek. Mine burned where he touched her. His youthful, racing enthusiasm was now replaced with a sadness that lay on his slightly stooped shoulders. His eyes occasionally caught mine as with a barbed javelin that held a hint of question I dared not answer.

My acting ability amazed me. Dinner, tea, and dessert went well, with Victoria chatting happily. I learned Victoria had met Dave when he led her study group to Rome for the university Victoria attended. I wondered about their meeting, but was due for another jolt.

Victoria cleared the tea cups then came up behind me, wrapping her arms around me. "Mother, we've saved the best news for last; we want to be wed here."

"Here?" was all that escaped from my closed throat.

Victor's look scalded me. What did it all mean?

SHADOWS OF NIGHT

Bedtime arrived early because the travelers were tired from their journey. As we three climbed the stairs into the pale light of the hallway and our separate rooms I caught Victor's lips moving as if telling me something over Victoria's back.

I crawled into bed and curled into a ball and once again let the tears well up. I knew Victoria would soon bound into my room and sit on the bed for girl talk. I tried to compose myself by opening the book on the Egyptian poison ring, trying to focus on something else.

Victoria showed Victor to the loft room on the third floor, then knocked on my bedroom door. "Mother, don't you just love him?" I tried to smile at her joy. "I knew it wouldn't surprise you he is so much older. I've always dated older men, my search for a father figure you always said, but I have to tell you one thing," she paused. "Dave isn't very well, something about the war, Agent Orange he says," her voice barely above a whisper. "So that's why we want to marry here, soon."

I breathed deeply.

"Mother, does the arm he lost in Vietnam upset you? I told him not to talk about the war, at least until I knew you wouldn't get upset thinking about my father."

"Your father," I managed to say.

"I know how desperately you loved my father, Mother. When I think of you it's always standing at the window looking out at the orchard. I knew you were thinking about him then."

"Yes, Victoria, I was." Sometime during those long lonely years my love for him must have changed. What did I feel now that he slept under my roof, the lover of his own unsuspecting daughter?

"Mother, you're shivering, it's late, I'll let you sleep now." She stepped from the bed. "I love you."

"And I you, Victoria, more than you will ever know."

She turned off the light and shut the door. I lay on my side in the darkened stillness for a long time. Then I heard the sound of the doorknob turning slowly.

VICTOR

Moonlight filtered through the lace curtains and came to rest on his bare feet. He stood for an eternity in that spot. The rest of him was in shadows. I studied those feet, remembered taking each toe into my mouth, sucking, nibbling, licking until he screamed stop and we rolled in giggles. A strange memory at a time like this. I no longer questioned the thoughts intruding on my sanity. I lay there, still and unmoving; still he stood studying me.

"Laurel," the sound of his voice was heavy. "Why, why, why?" The words came from deep within a tomb.

Sitting up I pulled the quilt close. In one giant step and he was beside me. The electricity charging the air made my breath stab my lungs.

"Is Victoria...is she my child?"

The stillness took on a force threatening to crush both of us. I nodded.

"Laurel, why didn't you let me know about Victoria? Why did it have to be this way? You-should-have-told-me," he hissed then leaned back. He gestured wide with his arm, then buried his head in his hand.

I leaned forward suddenly. "*I* should have told *you*? How? You seduced a sixteen-year-old girl then you ran out on me. You ran out on your wife. Ran out on life. All those years I waited, but never a word from you."

"I was going to find you after 'Nam, but everything just got harder and harder till I quit thinking about it."

"Like you forgot about everything that was hard," I gasped.

"Dammit Laurel, look at this." He moved the stump of his arm before my eyes. "I've had to live without an arm; how do you think that feels?"

"I had to live without you and Victoria without a father." I took a deep breath as the words poured from me. "I waited, Victor, I searched for your name in the lists of Vietnam casualties, I read every name on the list of missing, wounded, and dead. I prayed I wouldn't see Victor Mills listed. You never even looked for me, so spare me your pitiful whining."

"I went to serve my country. I lost my arm, I lost my wife, I lost you … all for honor."

"Honor! What honor? You preached brotherly love, but when things got too hot at home you ran. You didn't go to Vietnam for honor; you hid there among the heroes. That's why you went; you went to hide."

A sound close to a grunt escaped his lips as he fell toward me. His sobs shook the bed as his arm encircled my neck. "The Monsignor said he'd report me to the police because of you and I'd never teach again if I didn't enlist right then."

I pushed his twisted shape away; his tears dampened the gown which clung to my chilled breasts. "Did you expect a hero's welcome?"

He stood and stumbled toward the window. "No, Laurel, I didn't come home a hero. The heroes aren't the ones who came home from 'Nam, only sick shells like me." He turned to face me, shadows drawing deep furrows across his face. Stillness again, punctuated by his gulping breaths. "Laurel, I'm dying. Victoria knows I'm sick, but she doesn't know I've only got months to live." He dropped to his knees beside the bed. "Please, Laurel, it's too late for you and me. I beg you to let things go on with Victoria and me as we planned."

"Let you marry your own daughter?!"

"It's all I have left; she never has to know." A ray of hope lifted his voice.

"I'll see you dead before you defile our daughter and leave me again."

"Laurel," he lurched onto the bed. His hand reached out and the strength of his grip on my shoulder surprised me. "In 'Nam I killed. It never got easy but I did become efficient. No matter if it was the Cong or a villager. I could do it again. I won't let you ruin my last days by destroying the one thing I live for...the love in Victoria's eyes. Knowing about us would destroy her too. Think of your daughter."

"I am." The silence stretched. His grip on my shoulder became more, rather than less.

The moon crossed the distance and lit his face. I looked past his eyes into the torture chamber he once called soul. When his mouth covered my lips the tenderness surprised me. His body pinned mine until fear and passion began to churn in a madness that left only confusion and desire.

Hours later as I lay awake, I heard the creaks and groans of the house as if it were shuddering in disgust. With morning came the season's first snowflakes. Light and pure, they beat against the windows as if attempting to cleanse the dishonor that dwelled within.

When breakfast was finished, we took our coffee into the living room. A fire burned warmly as we sat down.

"Mother, you've been quiet this morning. Tell us about the antique store and the latest purchase you told me about, that Egyptian ring you're wearing this morning."

Victor sipped his coffee. His color matched the powder I'd stirred into his coffee mug.

"Oh yes, there's an ancient love ritual," I began, and then Victor moaned and fell forward, the coffee spewing across the rose print carpet.

GUILT AND ASHES

Through clenched teeth, Victoria said, "Mother, please." She held an ornately carved box. Her black dress and matching coat accented such pale skin. "Dave wanted to be cremated and his ashes tossed to the wind." Her deep blue eyes held steady. "Let me spread his ashes here. It will comfort me knowing his spirit roams free and Mother, he'll always be here with you."

Guilt touched with sadness threatened to overwhelm me. I'd poisoned the only man I'd loved since I was a young girl. I nodded. How could I argue with my grief-stricken daughter? She could never know this man, whose ashes she was going to release into my orchard, has lived here in my memories for most of my life and now he would be mine forever.

Victoria walked into the orchard. I watched her from the window as ghostly flakes slid down the frosty panes. Her hand caressed the parquet, mahogany box she clutched close to her heart. Carefully lifting the lid she dipped her trembling fingers into the ashy powder before a blast of frigid December wind lifted the feathery silt and flung it across the bleak orchard. I wished I could ease her pain as I watched the young woman close her eyes, lower her head, and whisper her final goodbye to the man she would never know was her father; the lover she had unknowingly delivered home to me. Later she insisted on leaving for school despite the swirling blizzard that encased the area. I naively believed my secrets were safe.

Today when Goldie and I walked the long road to town I wore boots and a warm coat. There was a thin coating of ice on the highway, so I waited until the county came by with the sand truck to walk into town. I've had an uneasy feeling since Victoria left. It's a feeling that makes me want to get away from the house and spend more time at the antique store. Guess I've got the jitters.

Last night as I stepped from the bathtub, I thought I saw Victor's face at the window. This morning when I looked toward the orchard, I saw a thin man disappear through the trees. One of the sleeves of his grey coat dangled empty. I hope Doug, my well-drilling friend, is around. Maybe tonight I'll let him give me a ride home and ask him in for a drink, so I won't have to be alone.

DOUG

Doug looked at Laurel sitting next to him in his pickup and smiled at the way she'd invited herself along for a ride home. He knew the woman as well as anyone could and wondered at her immediate need for his company. Maybe she wanted to hear about his two tours in Vietnam again. He didn't always want to talk about that time and the others who'd enlisted from the area. He liked to remember the first time he walked into the antique store and looked up at that hot redhead on a ladder. He'd heard about her, and knew she kept to herself, taking care of her Aunt Ruth and running the antique store. He'd heard she had a kid in boarding school some place. From what he could tell, she didn't date anyone in town. When she reached across a display the ladder had wobbled. He jumped over a wagon to grab her and set her down.

"You should be more careful on ladders."

She looked into his eyes and he felt a magnetic pull toward the unknown. Their friendship, if that's what it was, spanned many years, but never developed beyond their occasional coupling. He learned never to expect or wait for her. She wasn't like any woman he'd been with; he never knew when or if he'd see her again. When they were together, she confused him, even as she drew him into her.

That first day they left the antique store and came together with a need that echoed in their love sounds. Laurel leaned over Doug, her hair hid her face, her fingers trailed across his body like a teasing breeze that touched then retreated. When her right hand lifted the mass of russet waves from her face she leaned back, resting her hands on his knees.

"Sometimes my body and head and heart have different needs."

He waited for her next words. She waited for him to ask, but instead, she breathed deeply as she shifted atop his body. He had trouble relating to anything except what her body was saying to his.

"Doug, do you know what I'm telling you?" Her voice came in a hoarse whisper.

His hands roved across her breasts and to her shoulders. "*Ummm*," he groaned.

"For a woman, for me," she began moving her hips so he forgot her words and could only think of the heat in his groin. "Doug, my body is crying out for you." They began moving in unison. "But my heart," she panted, "my heart..."

He grabbed her shoulders to bring her mouth crushing down on his as he pushed deeper into her and their rhythm drowned their moans.

Doug understood a few things about her. Laurel wore silence like a sheer and clinging dress. She could wrap it around herself or shed it as desired, but the aura never really left her. It followed her and beckoned him to pursue. The way she wore secrets invited inspection, seduced speculation, and kept part of her out of reach. Doug waited for the times the silence would crack, shatter, and fall like ice from the branches of trees on a January morning. Laurel would turn, look into his eyes, and briefly lift the veil to give him a glimpse of the next layer. She flirted with, but never really drew him close enough to lay his heart against hers. Laurel wore an armor that surrounded her and barred his admittance to her secrets. She would turn away, never offering what he most wanted to hear. She captured a part of him that no longer belonged to him and he gave it without regret.

He often wondered what he left with her. Who held the key to Laurel's heart? What memories rested so deep within her that she ran when he ventured too close? But that first time he walked away feeling a new chapter was opening. Little did he know how little his life would intersect with hers. It was not as he had anticipated or hoped.

HISTORY REPEATING

Victoria drove from her mother's home on that snowy day feeling a deep unrest. She could still feel the gritty powder that was Dave's ashes. His death had opened some sealed door that beckoned her to learn more about this man she'd known a few short months but come to love deeply. She was relieved his ashes were in her mother's orchard.

There was something comforting yet disturbing about Dave and her mother's reaction to their visit. She wondered if it was his age, so much closer to Laurel's than hers, but all her boyfriends had been older. She supposed it was her search for a father figure, having grown up with only women. She dismissed the thought, but wondered if her mother had wanted Dave for herself. She had felt an undercurrent of something flowing between them.

Victoria wondered why so much of her life seemed to revolve around secrets and mysteries. She was an adult, but still didn't understand her own family. Why did she only hear about one set of grandparents? Didn't her father have parents? Laurel only spoke about the accident that took her parent's lives and how she looked like Laurel's mother, her grandmother. Victoria wondered if she'd ever learn why Laurel was so secretive about the past.

Within weeks of returning to school in January she began to suspect her morning nausea was because she was expecting Dave's baby. She wasn't yet sure of her feelings about things; so she began a search for Dave's background. His army foot locker was still in the trunk of her car. She gathered her courage and opened the lid. At the bottom was a school yearbook.

St. Genevieve? *Why would he have a yearbook from St. Genevieve?*

This was the school her mother and grandmother had attended. The year was 1967. She looked at the faces, read the names until she came to a photo she recognized; it was Laurel's photo. She was a sophomore, sixteen. *My mother was sixteen when I was born?* The story Victoria had been told growing up was different. The age her mother claimed to be was not true if she was sixteen in 1967; what did this mean? She paged further and found the faculty photos. There were nuns, lay teachers, and right there, Victor David Mills, her Dave. What did all this mean?

She called her mother.

"Victoria, I'm sorry, I don't recall a teacher at St. Genevieve named…" she paused, "David Mills. Certainly not the Dave you brought home."

"Not Dave, mother, it was Victor, Victor David Mills. How could you not know? St.

Genevieve was a small school and I saw your picture, you were sixteen."

There was silence from Laurel.

"Mother, you owe me an explanation about everything. Were you only sixteen when you had me? What about my father who was killed in Vietnam?" Victoria struggled to catch her breath. "Mother talk to me.

"It's quite simple, Victoria. Yes, I was 16 when you were born. I added two years because I was embarrassed, and your father was in Vietnam by then."

Laurel had planned what to say if this ever came up, but now feared Victoria would need more. So, she abruptly hung up saying a customer had come into the antique shop. It was a weak play for more time but the only one Laurel could come up with quickly.

Victoria felt there was more about the story her mother didn't and probably wouldn't talk about, so she headed to St. Genevieve to see if she could find some answers for herself.

On the way she reflected how she'd accepted the idea of being in St. Paul at boarding school once she began grade school. Her mother always encouraged her to bring friends home for long weekends and holidays. Now Victoria wondered if this was to avoid the mother-daughter talks she so desperately wanted? But she had loved bringing her friend's home where they'd scurry through the antique store and hide in all the cubby holes and tell each other ghost stories about the old furniture and costumes from past eras. Sunsets in the orchard were always a favorite with these friends. It was a fun time, but looking back, she wondered about her childhood and why her mother sent her away.

She drove the long trip to St. Genevieve with her brain whirling, arriving in the late afternoon. The ornate wrought iron gates opened to a long, tree lined drive leading to a cluster of red brick buildings.

In 1900, Jacob Marsh, with six winsome daughters to educate, deeded sixty-five acres to the Sisters of St. Joseph Carondelet. Named after his wife, Genevieve, the school still enrolled fifty new students each September as it had since opening in 1902.

Things had not changed much since the early days. The Monsignor who ran the school was a distant relative of Jacob Marsh. The girls still dressed in white blouses with plaid jumpers and berets. Most of the nuns were now modernized to include street dresses and a variety of hair colors protruding from their short veils. They still took their daily constitutional walk on the paths within the sixty-five-acre campus with their charges in tow.

Along with the school, the town boasted five bars, two churches, and the area's most modern implement company among other small businesses. The students remained on campus and were not exposed to the surrounding area except on Sundays when they attended Mass at St. George along with the local Catholics. During those Sundays the nuns kept a close watch on their charges, lest anyone stray so far as to eye any local farm boys.

LEARNING SECRETS - FINDING MORE

It was into these surroundings Victoria drove with a burning desire to discover more about the school both her mother and grandmother had attended and where Dave/Victor once taught history.

"Mother Superior, I wonder if you could give me information about a teacher you once employed? I'm doing research for a family reunion," Victoria stammered.

The rotund nun behind an oversized oak desk smiled, revealing two perfectly placed dimples. Opening the file cabinet next to her, she said, "Certainly dear, I've been here for thirty-five years and remember all of our teachers and even their birthdays. It's something the other nuns tease me about. Now who is it you are researching?"

"Mills, Victor David Mills."

The file cabinet slammed shut with a crash that moved the giant desk two inches.

"I'm sorry, but our files don't go back that far and we had a fire once and now if you'll excuse me I must get to chapel." With a burst of brown and white she disappeared through the door leaving Victoria standing alone in the dark paneled office. Her confusion grew.

Victoria left the office and began to wander the campus. Large stone buildings marked by signs that read Math, Science, and Gymnasium stood in a rectangle. With eyes drawn by a sign that said Art, Victoria entered a building that smelled like turpentine and oils. Gessoed canvases stood against one wall. Long tables with half-carved shapes stared back at her. From a corner she heard mumbling, then a scraping sound. She moved closer to discover a tiny woman wearing a dusty smock over an old-fashioned nun habit that obscured all but an intricately wizened face.

"Hand me that chisel," demanded the small woman. A brown, speckled hand shook as it grabbed the smallest of the chisels Victoria offered.

"Pretty smart, how did you know which one I needed?" asked the nun.

"I'm into art," was all Victoria said.

The nun turned her attention back to the cross she was carving. For long minutes Victoria marveled at the skill of the woman's bent and gnarled fingers as they fashioned an oak cross with her eyes closed.

"My eyes and hands give me some trouble, so I can only do this for an hour a day. Doctor said only a half-hour every other day. May as well shoot me as keep me out of the studio I say. So, Mother Agnes just turns the other way when she sees me heading for the studio," the little woman snickered.

"Sister, maybe you can remember a former teacher?" Victoria took a deep breath. "Victor David Mills?"

The nun laid the cross down and studied Victoria. "We don't talk about that time. I can't tell you any details."

"Please, Sister, he's dead now, so it can't matter anymore." Victoria held one of the bent hands in hers. The nun looked down at the smooth hand covering her own.

"Why do you want to hear that old story?"

"He is...was, close to our family," Victoria whispered.

After a deep sigh, the nun began. "Yes, he taught here, history. Oh, he was a good-looking man and all the girls were crazy over him. He got into trouble with that poor little red-headed girl. Her parents were killed when she was young. Mills was counseling her, we knew that, but didn't suspect what else he was doing until it was too late, and the damage was done."

Victoria remained silent as the nun continued her story.

"Once we learned what was going on the Monsignor had him shipped off to Vietnam." Victoria felt she couldn't breathe as she tried to assimilate the details she was learning. The nun continued, "Mills made it back I know, because he used to visit his war buddy, my cousin's boy, Ray. Ray Jones in Sunset. Ray lost use of his legs in the Vietnam war. I don't know what became of that little red-head girl." The nun turned back to her carving.

Victoria walked around the campus until she felt safe to drive, then checked the map and headed toward Sunset.

SUNSET

Spring broke records by arriving early that year. Snow disappeared as the crocus and daffodils appeared. Sunlight cut across the dirt road highlighting the dust that floated around Victoria as she slowly walked down the street leading toward the house the bartender told her belonged to Ray Jones.

The street was one of three that comprised the small town of Sunset, bordered by a heavily wooded area that rolled down toward the St. Croix River. At one time the bar/restaurant, now the only open business besides the auto shop, housed a thriving bank. That was when horse drawn wagons hauled lumber to Owens Landing as the mighty logs made their way downstream toward the Mississippi. Now many of the houses and businesses were boarded up or fallen down.

Victoria stepped around an empty five-gallon grease can as she neared a rusting mobile home. Her resolve to learn more about Dave's past seemed less important as she surveyed the sagging porch. Shading her eyes with her right hand, she held the porch support with her left and squinted into the dimness. A board creaked as someone shifted in the shadows.

"I'm looking for Ray Jones." Victoria stepped onto the porch. The spring sun glinted off a pile of discarded Walters beer cans.

A dry crackle of a cough punctuated by, "Yeah, what for?" came from the shadows.

"My name is Victoria."

"What can I do for you girl?" The voice rasped through the late day warmth. The chair creaked as the man shifted for a better view of the young woman. "Victoria, eh?" His look questioned as he studied her.

"I understand you were a friend of Dave, Victor David Mills, in Vietnam." As she moved forward her foot caught an empty beer can which rolled to the edge of the step and balanced in the silence before clattering to the ground.

"Dave? Hell yes." He began to laugh which ended abruptly. "Did you say were?"

"He died this winter, his heart." Her hand automatically touched her left breast.

"Damn, he was just here to visit me last, when was it? Must a been October. That's when, I remember cuz Larry, my younger brother, was here. He knew Dave too, but not like I did. I remember Dave said he wasn't feeling too good. That Agent Orange got us guys bad." He turned to look full on at Victoria. "You a relative?"

"Sort of, yes." Victoria swallowed and looked at the man in the wheelchair who studied her for a long time before his eyes moved to the street. The sun streaked through the screen and settled on his black turtleneck which showed the remains of some other day's meal. His mustache stretched across the lower half of a gaunt face.

"Sit down and I'll tell you about Dave. You really want to hear this?"

She stammered, "I think so." She wondered what this man would add to the strange picture that was emerging of her Dave. She was almost afraid to learn more but felt compelled to hear what Ray had to say.

"I'll tell you about..." He reached down and pulled a can of Walters beer from an opened case, retrieved a rusty opener that hung from a green nylon cord off the arm of the wheelchair, and offered her the opened beer.

"She doesn't want warm beer Ray." A voice, deep and clean, rolled from behind the screen door. The metal door swung open as a tall, muscular man with a neatly trimmed beard and mustache stepped out and offered Victoria a cold beer.

She could see they were brothers from the physical resemblance. Immediately she could feel the differences. Ray, in the chair, sat slumped, his head down, his fingers shook as he tapped a Marlboro from a crumpled pack of cigarettes. Ray's eyes were deep set and hooded. The other brother moved with loose, smooth motions. Victoria watched his body beneath jeans and a plaid shirt. His muscles gathered then relaxed as he moved to sit on the edge of the porch near her chair. His brown hair showed strands of silver. When he looked at her, his eyes held a warmth to match his smile.

"I'm Larry, Ray's brother. I knew Dave too, not as well as Ray; they were in the same platoon. I was still too young to join."

"You want to hear about Dave or not?" Ray took a long drink of warm beer and stared into the distance. "I guess it's time . . .

"It was '67 when my number got called up in the draft. #226. Our brother Greg got his notice day after he turned 18. His was #237, only eleven numbers apart. Hard to believe with all those numbers we'd pull numbers only eleven apart. There's five of us brothers. Three of us got drafted, but Ted, he went CO. That's conscientious objector. Larry, he was too young and Mack, hell I don't even remember why he didn't go. Greg and I were gone by that time." Ray shifted in his chair, but never looked toward Victoria or Larry.

After a deep breath, Ray went on, "Anyway, me and Greg were waiting for the bus in Center City. Ma, she's crying and Pa, he just keeps shaking his head. Up walks this guy with white hands. Ya, that's what I noticed first. Now me and Greg work hard and our hands are rough and callused. I could tell he was different from us; he made his living thinking, damn if I wasn't right. But turns out he wasn't a snob. He was…" Ray lifted his beer for a long sip. "He was scared, hell, we were all scared.

"When he told Ma he had no family, she started giving him cookies and gum for the trip. Yup, Dave went through basic with me. His hands got rough-looking like mine. They got that way in training, cleaning your weapon, crawling through cold mud. Dave was a lot tougher then he looked and had some pretty interesting stories he told me later...much later."

Victoria looked from one brother in the shadows on the porch to the other who sat on the step below her chair. The top of Larry's head tilted back toward her as he drank. She studied the thick brown, grey-laced hair as it swirled from a cowlick, the ends danced on the collar of his denim shirt. In silence the three tipped their beers. Larry crushed the can in his tanned fist before fetching two more from inside. Ray opened another warm one, balanced it on his leg. He took a breath which brought on a rasping cough, another breath, and he continued.

RAY REMEMBERS VIETNAM

With a nod Ray started the next part of his story, "We were embedded with South Vietnamese troops. We pushed deep into Cambodia, heading north to Laos. God, it'd been weeks of firefights, artillery, and assault teams back and forth between the Cong and us. Then we got support and mounted a big attack. We uncovered a North Vietnamese supply depot. We destroyed the village and watched inhabitants scatter as we moved north. We'd lose some of ours, replacements would arrive. Life went on, if you could call it that." Ray's eyes were closed, he leaned his head back.

Victoria shuddered and folded her arms around herself. Ray turned and his eyes fixed on hers. "It ain't' pretty, but it gets worse." Then he continued with a deep growl. "We went into this dirty, stinking village when a sniper hit one of ours. As he dropped, we spread out after the gooks. We caught the sniper and two others and by this time we were sick of shitheads shooting and spying. Well, Benson, a mean son of a bitch, he gets everybody riled up saying how these skinny little village runts should get what was coming to them. We lined up in two rows and as those slobs ran the gauntlet, we whipped um and beat um with our rifles. I remember Dave, at first he says how we can't do this. But by the time the guys are dead, hell, Dave's still beating on them and yelling like he's having the time of his life. We had to pull him off or he'd have kept it up."

Victoria looked straight ahead as Ray continued.

"It was just about then all hell broke loose. A round of mortars fell damn near on our asses. First thing gets hit is the radio so there's no way for us to call in support artillery. That meant we had to wait for Charlie Company to figure out why we missed our linkup and come looking for us. We dug in to wait, returning fire from our bunkers. We waited, Charlie Company didn't show that day and we were still waiting as it started getting dark. The mortars and rockets kept rolling in, sometimes light enough we'd think we could make a run for it, then *bam* they'd hit us with heavy rounds. That night the really bad shit happened."

Ray's chest started to move up and down as he gasped for air. Victoria moved toward him when Larry put his hand on her shoulder. "He's okay. Let him talk it through." Larry moved around her to open a warm Walters and place it in Ray's hand. His fingers curled around the can, then he bent to set it on the floor. His body came up and swayed back and forth as he returned to Cambodia and the hell that played on fresh in his mind.

"Nothing we could do but wait. Sitting in that damn foxhole waiting and smoking dope, waiting and smoking and soaked to the bone. All at once Dave jumped up and started to crawl forward. 'Where the hell do you think you're going you stupid fuck?' I asked Dave if he was going back to Wisconsin. His hands were covered in mud as he reached for the edge. I grabbed him and dragged him back down."

"'I have to get back to school, got to teach history,' Dave said. I told him, 'Cool it man, school's a long way off. You're acting weird. You've been smoking too much hash; it's making you crazy. We're all going crazy, so have a cigarette and sit down.' I figured Dave must have some kind of shell shock, so I'd keep him talking, maybe he'd come around. I asked him to tell me again about the titties on that little redhead he was banging at the girl's school where he taught. Then Dave jumped up again, I reached for him and hung onto his pants leg as he tried to climb over the side of the bunker." Ray's breathing came in shallow gasps.

"Then it happened, a round hit. I saw Dave's arm explode. There was blood on both of us when another round hit and I flew backwards.

Neither of us made a sound during those ten seconds, then I heard Dave making sort of a howl as he stared where his arm was all bone and blood. You couldn't see much in the gloom until a round flashed and then it was so bad you can never forget.

"After I got hit everything went numb. I thought it was the shock, I couldn't move my fucking legs. I tried to drag myself toward Dave who sat there moaning and staring at the bone pieces sticking out of his arm. 'Dave, help me, I can't move my legs. I need to get a tourniquet on your arm before you bleed to death. Medic!' I screamed, 'need a medic.'

"Then Dave rolled toward me, 'Ray, my arm, my arm,' he gasped. The medic crawled over to us and got Dave's bleeding to stop. He looked at my wound and gave both of us morphine before he moved on to others who'd been hit. We passed out, don't know how long. We shook awake as a round hit Meyer's foxhole.

Meyer screamed for fifteen minutes before everything got quiet until the next round."

Ray bent forward as tears coursed down his haggard face. After a long silence he raised his head and went on.

"'Dave, Dave,' I asked, 'you still here?' 'Yeah Ray, I'm alive.' Dave murmured back to me." Ray twisted in his chair. He was no longer telling Victoria the story, he was back in that bunker in Cambodia.

"We'd slip in and out of consciousness. The medic checked and gave us more morphine. 'Ray, if I die, do me a favor, tell my wife I'm sorry. Will you do that for me Ray? And Laurie, Laurel you know it's her fault, and the Monsignor, they, they sent me here to die…' Old Dave was bawling and kept mumbling something that made no sense. Suddenly he said, 'Ray, I gotta get help. You gotta round in your back, my arm's shattered, Luke over there is bleeding out and Meyer, he's screaming for fifteen fucking minutes for his ma. Radios down so I've got to get us help.'

"'Don't be stupid, Dave, it's death out there.' But Dave stumbled to his feet like he didn't hear me and tried to shoulder his rifle but dropped to his knees as the pain shot through his body and he begged to die. 'Hey Dave, you dumb son of a bitch, you aren't going to fucking die and neither am I. I gotta see my brothers and…quiet, Dave do you hear that?'

"There it was, the hum and whump, and then six Hueys on the horizon. I grabbed Dave's good arm and told him neither one of us was going to die cuz we had to get home to Sunset for our hero's welcome."

Ray bent forward as tears rained down his haggard face into his mustache. He wiped his face on the sleeve of his shirt. After a long silence he raised his head and went on.

"When Dave was here, I asked if he ever saw his little redhead again. He said no, but last time I saw him here he was in love, called her

Victoria. That's you, right?" Ray turned his red-rimmed eyes to the stricken woman whose arms were wrapped around her as she rocked back and forth in the metal lawn chair.

Ray's cough ripped the evening air. Larry sat in silence.

"Meyer, he's still screaming. Sometimes at night when I wake up with the sweats, I hear him. I get out of bed and into my wheelchair and roll to the door, but when I open it the screams stop. Just like they did that time in 'Nam. Meyer, he's not the only one who's screaming."

Ray slumped deeper into his chair. The beer sat on the warped, wooden, porch floor ignored. The Marlboro he'd lit earlier was cold and twitched between his gnarled fingers. The war continued with the ghosts that fought and now dwelled within him.

He threw back his head. "Larry, I'm going to bed." Without a word Larry got up, turned the wheelchair, and pushed his brother through the screen door.

AFTER RAY'S STORY

Twilight lingered on the porch with Victoria. She heard Ray's voice in her head repeat the name: *Laurel.* Her mother? Dave? After this and what the nun at St. Genevieve told her, there was no doubt about the connection between her mother and Dave or Victor; yet a million questions swirled in her head.

A light came on and pushed through the window, spotlighting her. She heard water run and the toilet flush. Turning her head, she watched through the window as Larry lifted his brother and placed him gently on the bed. Numb, she waited until the light was turned off, then stood.

Larry moved through the darkness and stood close to her. There was enough of the new moon to outline his face. They stood together in silence. He put his hands on her shoulders, then folded her weeping body close to his heart. "Victoria, do you want to walk down to the river?" She held her hand out to him as they left the porch and wandered slowly through the town and down a path leading to the river.

"Did that answer your questions about Dave?"

"Yes, too many," she sighed.

They sat on the sand and watched the river in silence until he explained how the brothers took turns every two weeks staying with Ray. He began to tell stories of growing up and playing at the river.

Victoria listened and managed to laugh at some of his tales. Slowly she warmed and talked to him about her days at the boarding school. Finally, she told him of her suspicions about Dave and her mother, but she wasn't ready to talk about the child she carried in her womb. He listened without comment then he took her hand

and placed it against his lips, helping her up the bank they returned to Sunset.

Larry covered Victoria and sat next to her on the sofa as her breathing slowed. He had questions about this lovely girl now asleep on the sofa in the trailer. He'd never heard Ray tell about Dave in Vietnam. He had more questions about the secrets between Laurel and Dave and this emotional girl asleep on the sofa. He wanted to wake her for answers but realized the answers he got might lead to more questions. She was so young, and Dave was Ray's age. After the story Ray told he wondered about the connections. Somehow, he felt caught in a web that seemed to have ensnarled all of them.

Victoria stayed in Sunset trying to forget about her mother and Dave and their betrayal. She kept going back to the secrets they'd harbored for so long. She slept on the sofa. Down the hall Larry stretched out on the bed each night thinking about this beautiful, sad woman tossing on the sofa. Ray watched them both, saying little.

She knew she would soon leave to confront her mother about the truth she'd learned, but not yet, not while she felt so safe and where she felt secure amidst the turmoil of her life.

She spent her days at the river painting, organizing Ray's trailer and making suppers they'd share just like a family when Larry got home from work.

"Victoria, do you like to dance?" Larry finished the last dish and turned the dishpan over to drain. She tossed the towel to him and began to dance around the kitchen.

"Oh yes, looks like the lady loves to dance," said Ray looking up from his place in front of the television in the living room.

"Let's walk over to the Banker's Hours bar. There's a band playing tonight from Lindstrom. Ray, want to wheel over with Victoria and me?"

"Maybe I'll roll over later," Larry mumbled from in front of the television.

Victoria finished bathing and was buttoning her white blouse when Larry appeared at the door and watched her. Victoria's light hair swirled out from her head and with the light shining through from the bathroom it looked like cotton candy. She smiled and turned to the mirror to pull her hair into a pony tail tied with a black ribbon. He studied her from the doorway. Her tall frame hid traces of a changing body, except for the full breasts that played against the top of her scoop neck blouse. Larry's hands longed to reach for her and press her close. But instead, he picked up the towel and hung it over the door knob.

"Let's go dancing pretty lady." He pulled her into the dusty street which was dark except for truck lights that crisscrossed the street as they pulled into parking places by the bar. The door to the Banker's Hours was open allowing a sweet country tune to lick at their ears. The burly voice of the singer pulled them through the door as he sang about lost loves and spilled beer.

"Larry, this your new gal? Heard you had a pretty one staying with you." A round man wearing wide suspenders and holding a pitcher in one hand and a beer glass in the other smiled at her. "Grab a couple of glasses, I'll share." He hoisted the pitcher.

"Victoria, this is Carl Meyer, his brother is the Meyer that Ray told you about from Vietnam."

"My brother got killed in Vietnam," the big man said as if these were words were still new.

More folks strolled over to meet the beautiful blonde with Larry. They easily accepted her place among them. She watched the exchange between Larry and the others. She saw the serious look of concern on his face during conversations about a farmer's sick cow, the construction business, and the latest storms. "Half the folks here are my cousins," said Larry in response to a questioning look on her face.

"Grandpa had nine brothers and sisters, so damn near everybody in these parts is related."

"You aren't like Ray or most of them," Victoria looked into his eyes.

"And you, are not like any gal I've ever been with."

The music changed from a rollicking two-step to a soft, swaying, tender-touching melody. Larry gathered Victoria into his arms leaving Meyer still talking about the new irrigation system he was installing.

Slowly the song began. A woman's voice filled the dim air with the pleasure of returning memories. Like a tide that encircled and washed the faces of the partners gazing at their dreams. The singer closed her eyes and invited the dancers into their own secret memories.

We met one year on the twelfth of June
It was a civilized love affair,
Till the lights went out and you took down
The ribbons from my long hair.
Never met a man who could bare my soul
And leave my body untouched
Or touch my body and devour my soul
The way you did on the twelfth of June.

The music moved the dancers as they swayed closer. Victoria felt the warmth of Larry's body through her sweat-soaked shirt. The fingers of his hand moved ever so slightly on her back, drawing her closer. Aware of every inch of his body pressed close to hers, it was like a strange new part of herself with only desire between them. She was afraid to move and lose this moment. Her heart beat faster, echoing his as they leaned into the rhythm. His hand reached into her hair and pulled it free of the ribbon which fluttered to the floor just as the singer repeated:

Till the lights went out and he took down
The ribbons from my long hair.

"Victoria, I want to be alone with you."

"Yes," she whispered in his ear.

They were stopped by several friends as they made their way to the door. The small talk seemed infuriating to them. Outside they walked into the darkness and stopped.

"Home?" he asked.

"The river."

They returned to the same place they'd been the first night she arrived. They stood at the shore; Larry kicked at a rock that scuttled into the churning water. A fallen log caught the current and sent it twirling away from them.

"Victoria, I want to make love with you, but I don't know if you're ready. And if I make love to you it won't be casually, I don't feel that way about you."

"I'm still going to search for answers about Dave that I can't find here. But right now is our time Larry. I want to make love with you too, but there's something I have to tell you first." Victoria took a deep breath and began. "I didn't know my mother and Dave had any connection. I was going to marry Dave. I was in love with him. Now I'm having his baby and I'm lost. I don't know what to do about this baby. I need to confront my mother and decide what to do."

Larry watched her, studied her face as questions raced through his mind about how their feelings could grow, how they might overcome this unusual circumstance. They looked at each other for minutes before a smile touched Larry's lips and his hand caressed her cheek.

They reached toward each other and spilled onto the warm sand. Touching and tasting, their bodies flowed in rhythm with the currents of the river. The moon watched, then discreetly ducked behind a cloud as the sounds of their lovemaking carried downstream.

For the next few nights she lay beside Larry, feeling the length of his body pulled close to hers. When she sat up to move away his arms opened and she fell back against him, turned her face into the silken hair on his chest. She still struggled to understand or forget about her mother and Dave, but while being with Larry her mind was given a rest, and pleasure, and comfort. His tenderness surprised her. His gentle strength, coupled with his acceptance, healed her troubled mind and soul.

The morning sun was barely up when Larry stepped out of the shower before dressing for work. Victoria was packing her things.

"I knew one of these days you'd be going. Sort of hoped you could stay through next Saturday; my cousin's wedding." He held tightly to the towel around his waist.

She smiled at him and turned away. "Tell Ray goodbye." She didn't trust herself to look at him. Although his face smiled, his eyes had looked sad when he'd seen her packing. Her chest hurt, as if her heart was pounding to escape. She wanted to rush into his arms, to stay safe forever. If she looked at him standing there with water dripping off his hair onto his shoulders, she knew she wouldn't be able to leave so she moved quickly toward the door.

"Wait, Victoria, my address up north. I know you've got things to do now, but if you get up north when I'm not working construction, you'll find me there in my carpenter shop." He handed her a slip of paper.

She reached her hand out for the paper with his address and placed it carefully in her bag. She had to say something. Tears danced in her eyes and her body ached. "Larry," she reached out her hand. "Thank you." She touched his arm as she pushed past him.

He watched her from the doorway. She sat in her car for a moment, trying to remember how to start it. Even this simple task seemed hard. It felt like years since she'd first driven into Sunset. She checked the mirror, expecting to see an aged woman. She put the car in gear and slowly drove away. Why was she leaving? Why did she tell Larry about Dave's baby? Why was she heading back to Clover and her mother's house for more lies and deceit?

BACK TO LAUREL

Victoria phoned me. "Mother, I'm coming home to talk to you; I need answers."

My breath caught and the silence spread. "Of course darling, come home," I whispered. I hung up; my fear of what Victoria had learned about the past loomed before me. But perhaps this was to be just a visit.

All day I couldn't stop myself from going to the window that looks out into the orchard and beyond to the road, expecting to see Victoria's car. When she arrived we moved to the living room and sat down. She began without preamble or chatter.

"Mother, tell me about Dave and you and your time at school. I learned some things at St. Genevieve and from Ray in Sunset."

What did Victoria mean about Ray? How did she know him? Was this the Ray in Sunset I'd tracked down? The veteran who'd lost use of his legs in Vietnam? The Ray who was a war buddy of Victor?

I'd found him and intended to talk to him soon after the funeral, but when I got to Sunset and stopped in front of his house, I drove away. I was afraid of what he might tell me. What had Ray told Victoria?

I sat frozen as I planned what I could say about that time. My head was spinning. My planned responses lost to me. Before I could answer she said, "Is Dave, I mean Victor David Mills, my father?" A sound like a hiccup escaped her throat.

I had tried so hard over the years to cover my past so it wouldn't interfere with her life and in doing so had delivered her into confusion and pain. I stared in horror at the truth now looming before me. I grabbed the photo of the stranger soldier I'd passed off as her father for all the years.

"Victoria, here is your father."

My angry daughter grabbed the photo from my hand and in the scuffle, it fell and the glass broke. Shattered pieces of glass lay covering a second photo that I'd wedged behind the soldier picture. It was the only photo I had of Victor. I'd taken it in my bedroom and his young seductive smile now stared at both of our stricken faces.

I reached for her hand, which she yanked back. It was now grasping the photograph of Victor close. I had to tell her something about our past, about what life was like during the war. "Yes, Victoria it is time." I took a breath and began.

"I don't know if you or your generation can understand this. The war has been over for almost twenty years. I didn't go, many of us didn't have fathers or brothers or sisters who served. It didn't matter if we knew anyone or not. Because of that war, we grieve, our whole generation; those of us who were young in those days remember all too well. But then, when we were young, we isolated ourselves behind our small and fuzzy TV screens. We watched, we read, we discussed the war. But our lives went on…all the while other lives of young men and women didn't. They died by the hundreds of thousands or rotted in prison camps and we went on." Laurel took a shaky pause.

"My generation smoked dope on Friday nights and listened to the Moody Blues and bought baby food, and junk food, and rode bikes, and philosophized about that war. All the while others beat their way through jungles and had their bodies blown to bits and lost eyes and limbs and lives and rotted away in Vietnam."

Victoria exhaled and sat looking at me. "Why are you telling me this now, Mother? You never talked about any of this. But what about Dave? What does all this have to do with you and Dave?"

I continued without looking at my daughter. "When some of them came home from the hell that was the war, some who never went to fight turned their backs on them and called them traitors. *We* were the traitors. At night when I can't sleep, I walk into the orchard and I cry for them; for those who went and did their duty and I cry for us who stayed home and failed to do ours.

"Someday Victoria, I'll go to the Wall to thank them. I can't go yet, but someday I'll go alone at sunrise and I'll kneel down in front of that granite wall and beg their forgiveness. I'll thank the soldiers, everyone...the ones who volunteered and the ones who got drafted, the ones who led and those who followed. I cry for the ones who found their way back and those who will always be missing and the ones here with their souls stretched thin and their livers corroded from booze and drugs because they still can't leave the war behind. I'll kneel and thank them for myself and for my generation."

Victoria turned toward me. "And what about me, Mother? Will you ask my forgiveness for the years of lies and deceit? Mother, answer me!"

I couldn't look at Victoria. I got up and went to the window and pressed my forehead against the pane. I heard broken glass crunching as she walked out of the room and out of my life. I couldn't admit to her that Victor was her father. He was mine and mine alone. Victoria would never understand.

VICTORIA HEADS NORTH

The hot spell that autumn broke records. The south shore of Lake Superior sweltered. Locals gathered at the bar and marina to swap stories of how they couldn't remember it being this hot so late in the year. The big black flies that lit and stabbed into chunks of exposed flesh were worse than anyone could recall.

It was into this heat that Victoria arrived, months before her baby was due. She clutched Larry's address in her hand as she fought to see through the bugs on her windshield.

She'd planned to have an abortion. At the doctor's office they discussed birth defects due to an older father, and Agent Orange exposure. She couldn't bring herself to talk about the complex family relationships. When the tests confirmed a healthy baby, she couldn't go through with the abortion. So she made plans to have the baby in Milwaukee then give it up for adoption in this city where she had no connections. She'd driven there, gone to check out the hospital. It was during a conversation with staff arranging the adoption that she bolted. She got into her car and drove straight to Blue Wave.

She clutched the little bit of paper Larry had pushed into her hand when she left Sunset. She didn't know where else to turn. The number in Sunset was disconnected so she had headed north.

Now she was driving into the little town of Blue Wave. The population sign read 250 inhabitants. She followed Main Street toward the lake. The marina building faced the lake, windows on each side brightened the interior which was decorated with boating equipment and scenic tee shirts for sale.

She asked directions to Larry's cabin from a man in a rocking chair who began a litany of stories about Blue Wave and its history. Victoria ducked into the bathroom where she washed her face and attempted to unsnarl her wind-blown hair.

Back in the car, she drove across a bridge that spanned a weed-filled creek. The dust from an old pickup heading toward her choked the inside of her car. She slowed to pass a mobile home with two older folks sitting in aluminum lawn chairs; they seemed oblivious to the dust. Across the road, three men leaned against a grey pickup; an open twelve-pack sat on the tailgate of the truck.

At a Y in the road she turned right and headed through an open wooden gate. Victoria drove a quarter mile on a tree-lined path with grass growing down the middle. The house appeared as she rounded a curve. Weathered cedar covered the one-story house bridged to another building by a roofed breezeway. Several screened outbuildings stood in the distance. A low-slung red car and Larry's pick-up were parked side by side east of the house.

Victoria parked next to the truck and stared at the picturesque view of the mighty lake. Lake Superior was so expansive that no opposite shoreline was visible from that point. A huge woodpile and rock fireplace stood at one side of the house. A row of shells and interesting rocks and twisted driftwood lined the low wall which wrapped around two sides of the house and deck. Victoria hefted herself from the car and inhaled the sweet smell of pine trees and clean, fresh air.

"Can I help you?" inquired a female voice.

Victoria looked up to gather in a pair of long, tanned legs topped by a pair of very short blue shorts. She stared at the woman with the long legs but couldn't think of what to say. When she opened her mouth to respond, nothing came out.

"Sandy, who's here?" Larry emerged from around the house; in his hand he carried a saw.

Victoria started toward him then crumbled on the ground at his feet.

"Larry, what the hell is going on? Who is this woman? You owe me an explanation," Sandy demanded as Larry carried Victoria toward the house. "Is this why we never got together in Sunset? Did you get this woman pregnant? What about me and our relationship?" She followed him into the house still complaining.

Larry placed Victoria on the sofa. "Come outside with me, Sandy."

When they closed the door behind them Larry took a breath and began the hard conversation he'd been too cowardly to tackle since he'd returned from Sunset. Sandy's eyes filled with tears. She looked at him for a long time, turned and without comment, got into her car and drove away.

He didn't feel good about how he'd treated Sandy. And now a harder conversation faced him.

Victoria was sitting on the sofa when Larry came inside. He looked at her then brought her a glass of water. She sipped the cool liquid and said, "I'm sorry, Larry, I'm really sorry, I didn't know where to turn." Tears began to spill down her face.

"Are you alright? Is your baby coming right now?" The frantic look on his face caused Victoria to smile through her tears.

"I guess I have driven too long and eaten too little for the baby's comfort. They let you know if you do something they don't like." Her hand rubbed her swollen belly. She turned to survey the room, then hesitated, "Is that woman with the long legs still here?"

A half smile played across Larry's face. "Sandy left. I guess the sight of a pregnant woman collapsing at my feet was a bit much for her."

Now silence surrounded them. Then they both began to talk at once then stopped. Their gazes locked as each studied the other's eyes, searching for questions that had no answers at the moment. Victoria broke the silence as she looked across the room at a hand-carved stool against the wall. "Does she live here with you?" She couldn't look at Larry.

"Sometimes."

"I thought you said you aren't casual about love."

"It's not really love, but I did consider it casual, she's been here off and on for the past three years."

"Why did she leave?"

Larry stood and walked to the large window that framed a view of gentle waves for as far as the eye could see. "She leaves occasionally. When she figures that I'm never going to marry her, then she leaves. I never told her I would, just figured maybe someday I'd feel more for her and it would just happen. But after

Sunset I knew what it felt like to really love. Then you were gone. Now you show up here and everything's changed again." He took a breath and turned toward her. "Why are you here, Victoria? Why now?" The light behind him made his face disappear in shadows.

She took a deep breath then stood looking up at him. "I came to be with you, Larry. I want you to be the father to this child. I tried to get rid of it; I tried to give it up for adoption, but I can't. The baby is...Dave's ah, Victor's baby. I belong to this baby and it to me and I want you to be a part of us. If you will." She dropped her head and stood waiting for his refusal.

"Marriage too?" he asked as tears filled her eyes and her nose ran. She searched her pocket for a tissue. Finding none, she lifted the hem of her top and wiped her nose. Her eyes looked down at her bare feet caked with dirt between the toes. She sobbed.

"That's a lot to think about, Victoria." He paused a long time before continuing. "I hoped you'd come. All these months I looked for you. Why did you wait?" His voice came out in a rasp. "You told me about this baby in Sunset, but then I didn't hear from you and now…"

She lifted her head, straightened her back and searched for her sandals as she turned and started toward the door.

"Victoria, you can't leave yet, we need to talk, you need to eat something, the baby needs food. You can stay here until we figure things out." He moved across the room to the far end of the home to a tidy, well-stocked kitchen. Larry opened the refrigerator, then turned. "Go ahead and take a shower if you want, I'll make something for us to eat."

Victoria wasn't sure what to do. She felt confused and thought coming here was a mistake.

"Victoria, you can't leave yet. Please don't leave. We'll figure this out."

She was exhausted, craved food, and a shower.

The bath was sided in cedar with a skylight that sent soft afternoon light into the oversized glass-enclosed shower. Victoria cried as she scrubbed and shampooed. She felt foolish for coming here and expecting Larry to welcome her without question. The soap slipped from her hand when she jumped after hearing a knock and then the door opened.

Larry's long body edged through the steam as he opened the shower door and reached for the soap. Turning her around he rubbed the pine-scented soap over her shoulders. The suds ran down her swollen breasts. His hands followed and continued to roam over her belly and down between her legs. She leaned her head back against his chest and closed her eyes letting the water cascade over her face.

"Yes." He breathed against her neck. "Stay Victoria, I want to be with you forever."

She breathed deeply. "Are you sure you want both of us? Me and Victor's child?"

She turned to face his smile. They exchanged a long look then she turned him around. She rubbed the soap between her hands and across his back; her hands caressed his buttocks. He leaned his head against the wall and moaned as her hands moved around to the front of his body. His breathing came in gasps as she slipped around to face him. He wrapped his arms around her and pulled her as close as her stomach would allow while their lips touched hungrily.

The water turned cool then cold as beads of steam rolled down the shower walls and pooled on the floor.

LAUREL
THREE YEARS LATER

When Victoria walked out that day, I didn't see her for three years. Eventually she wrote to me and our correspondence began. I became aware of her life with Larry in Blue Wave after he retired from the construction business in Sunset. I eagerly waited for each letter with updates about their boy, Donny, my only grandchild. One day I received a special letter.

Dear Mother,

It has been so long since we've seen
each other. Donny, is going to have a
brother or sister. Larry and I feel
Donny needs to meet his grandmother
in person, not just in letters.

Donny wonders if you will bake cookies
together. Our visit will be in the fall
when tourist season is over.

Victoria's letter went on about the business she and Larry had begun together. I never inquired if they drove back to Sunset to visit Larry's brother Ray. I thought of visiting him myself, but I was afraid to learn more than I already knew about Victor.

What did their visit mean? Did Victoria still blame me for what happened in the past? I felt nervous as I awaited the day.

Victoria and Larry finally arrived one fall day when the leaves swirled down from the trees and across the road. I watched as a deep burgundy, newer model pickup truck pulled up to park between the house and orchard.

I watched Larry unfold a set of long, muscular legs from the truck. His hair was mostly grey and caught on the collar of his jacket. Then Victoria alighted. She wore a full skirted, tie-dyed dress that pulled tight over her pregnant belly. Her coat flapped in the wind. Her hair was pulled back and tied with a sage green ribbon, much as I have long worn my own hair. I warmed as I watched Larry's broad hand reach out to caress Victoria's cheek and then his arm tightened around her shoulders as if to lend courage to her. At that moment I felt entirely alone.

Then I saw *him* emerge from the truck.

Donny.

I was finally going to meet my grandson. My heart raced as I reached for the door. "Victoria," my voice broke as we embraced. I dropped to my knees in front of the child. I studied his dark hair and slight build, but it was when he looked into my eyes that everything seemed to stop in place. His eyes, intense, deep blue, were Victor's eyes. I had assumed Larry was the boy's father, but here was Victor, young Victor staring back at me. Victoria must have been pregnant the last time I saw her. Did it happen the night she brought Victor back to me?

I looked up and saw Victoria watching me. Her expression was fixed. I saw pain and something else. It was as if she was telling me I wasn't the only one with secrets. Her look issued a challenge I couldn't understand. How much did she know about the past? My mind was churning.

After lunch, Larry and Victoria left to visit Ray, who was now in a nursing home. Donny stayed with me for the afternoon.

I know I was fussing over him, but couldn't stop. "Donny, would you like to put together a puzzle?" I'd brought some enchanting old puzzles and games from the antique store to entice him. I studied the child as he bent intently over the pieces scattered across the table. I fancied there was a hint of my red in his dark hair.

"Grandma, look," he said, as he fit the last piece in place and turned his intense look my way.

"Come Donny, get your jacket," I said as I buttoned my coat. I took his hand and led him into the orchard. After all, it was time for him to meet his grandfather and father. We'd talk to Victor.

I pulled the boy close as we settled onto the garden bench to wait for Victor.

"I don't see anyone," the boy looked around.

"*Shh*, he's here. He visits me here in the orchard. Close your eyes and just wait."

THE END

ABOUT THE AUTHOR

Sharon Durken has published stories, articles, and poems in newspapers and magazines in a number of states, even a quilting publication in Japan has showcased her work. Durken is an active member of writing groups in Wisconsin, Minnesota, and Arizona, and past president of High Desert Branch of the California Writers Club. One of her poems was selected for inclusion in the 2018 Ariel Anthology. Several of her song lyrics are being produced by a Nashville musician.

Durken lives in a log cabin in northern Wisconsin. She has two sons, a Golden Retriever named Hannah, and Maine Coon cat, Pompeii. When not writing, she travels, quilts, and teaches rug making classes.

When asked where she gets inspiration for what she writes: "From people, places, experiences and imagination,"she answers.

The author of Hero's Welcome has lived in a number of interesting countries and states, including three years in Germany. She is currently working on a Civil War poetry book and a novel set in the 1860s.

59202916R00071

Made in the USA
Columbia, SC
02 June 2019